For my parents, Pete and Tracy

MIX
Paper from
responsible sources
FSC® C002795

Imelda and the Goblin King © Flying Eye Books 2015.

This is a first edition published in 2015 by Flying Eye Books,
an imprint of Nobrow Ltd. 62 Great Eastern Street, London, EC2A 3QR.

Text and illustrations © Briony May Smith 2015.
Briony May Smith has asserted her right under the Copyright,
Designs and Patents Act, 1988, to be identified as the Author of this Work.

Published in the US by Nobrow (US) Inc.

ISBN: 978-1-909263-65-9

Order from www.flyingeyebooks.com

Imelda & the
GOBLIN KING

Briony May Smith

Flying Eye Books

London - New York

There was once a girl called Imelda and all her life she had lived next to a wood.

But this was no ordinary wood, because among the whispering trees and enchanted groves, a fairy queen and her friendly fairy-folk dwelled.

Every day, Imelda would race to the enchanted forest
to play with the fairies and learn of its many secrets.

There was nothing lovelier than a day spent with the fairies.

Until one day a great, big, nasty bully arrived...

STOMP, STOMP, STOMP
came the sound of

THE GOBLIN KING!

Within moments of
his arrival the goblin king
and his goblin horde had
frightened away the fairy folk.
They couldn't understand
why he was so angry!

One day, the fairy queen wondered, scary as the goblin king was,
if they were kind to him then maybe he would be kind to them too?

The fairies all agreed to invite him to the fairy solstice.
After all it was a very important celebration!

The day of the fairy solstice arrived and the goblin
king came, but the fairies kindness seemed to have made
no difference. His scowl was as sour as ever...

...and so were his manners! The fairies could only watch
in astonishment as the goblin king gobbled up the whole feast.
Every plateful, every mouthful, every crumb!

The goblin king towered above the fairy queen in
fury. No one told him what to do! He leapt to his feet
and smashed up the feast and grabbed the queen.

He carried her off deep into the woods and imprisoned her in a cage.

The fairies were horrified and begged the goblin king to let their queen go. He ignored their cries and ordered the goblins to chase them away. The fairies knew there was only one person who could help them.

When Imelda heard what had happened she called all her fairy friends together and asked them what they knew about the goblin king. It was clear enough that the goblin king wasn't sharing the forest with anyone, and before long they had come up with a plan.

A pie would be baked, half of it with blue berries and half with red ones.
If the goblin king was nice, and ready to share, Imelda would slice him a piece
from the blue side, and he'd be fine. But if he was mean and greedy he'd
eat the whole lot, red berries and all...

With the freshly baked pie, Imelda and the fairies
sped through the trees. They ran deeper and deeper into
the woods until they reached the goblin king's lair.

The greedy goblin king laughed. The pie looked too delicious
to resist. He grabbed the pie and gobbled it all up in one bite.

I DON'T SHARE!

His stomach began to gurgle and all at once he looked rather ill.

He gawked at Imelda with bulging eyes as his body began to shrink and change. He cried out and just like that he was transformed into...

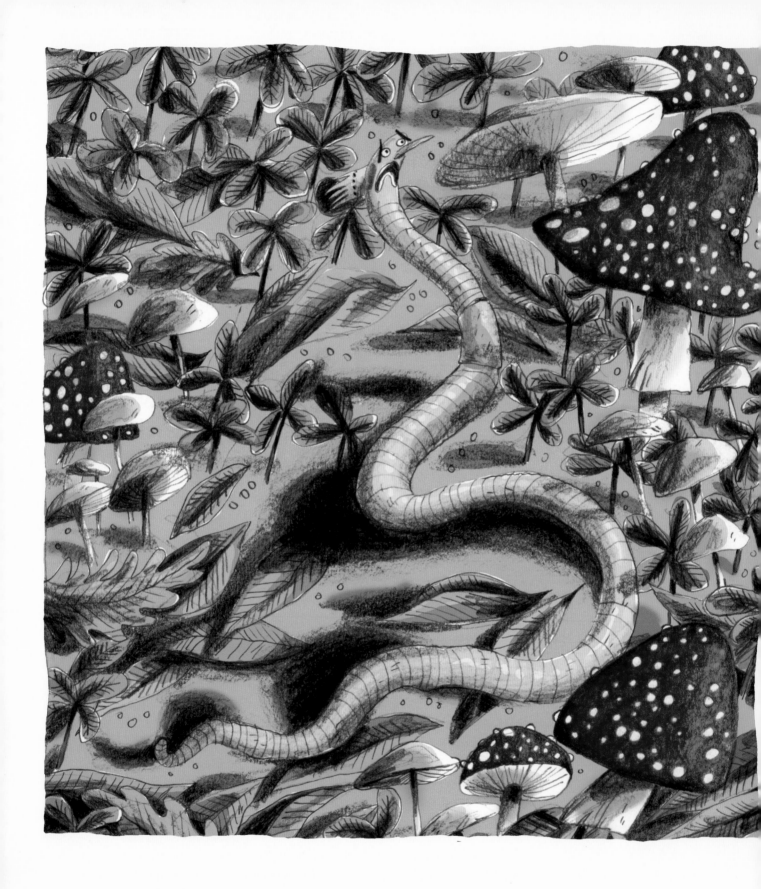

... a wriggling, squiggling, puny, little worm!

Imelda smiled triumphantly. The little goblins were free!
They all cheered as they presented the goblin king's crown
of oak leaves to their new queen.

From then on, no one ever feared the nasty goblin king's

STOMP, STOMP, STOMP!

The bully was gone and the forest folk could happily
share the forest together, with the Queen of the Fairies
and Queen Imelda of the Goblins ruling side by side.